First published 2013 by
Mabecron Books
42 Drake Circus
Plymouth
PL4 8AB

Illustrations Rebecca Cobb
Designed by Peter Bennett

Typeset in Garamond 3
Printed in Malaysia

ISBN 978 09572 5601 9

For Amber & Blake

THE LONELY
SEA DRAGON

HELEN DUNMORE

ILLUSTRATIONS BY REBECCA COBB

Mabecron Books

The Sea Dragon was lost,
and he hid in a dark cave,
weeping blue and green sea dragon tears.

He was all alone and his tears made
a deep pool in the sand.
'I'm lost! I'm lost!' sobbed the Sea Dragon.
'I've lost all my friends and relations!'

Amy and Callum were playing in the rock pools when they heard the Sea Dragon crying. Bravely and boldly, they went into the cave, and there he was.

'Don't cry,' said Amy, and she patted his beautiful scales. 'We'll be your friends,' said Callum, and he showed the Sea Dragon the little crab that was swimming in his bucket.

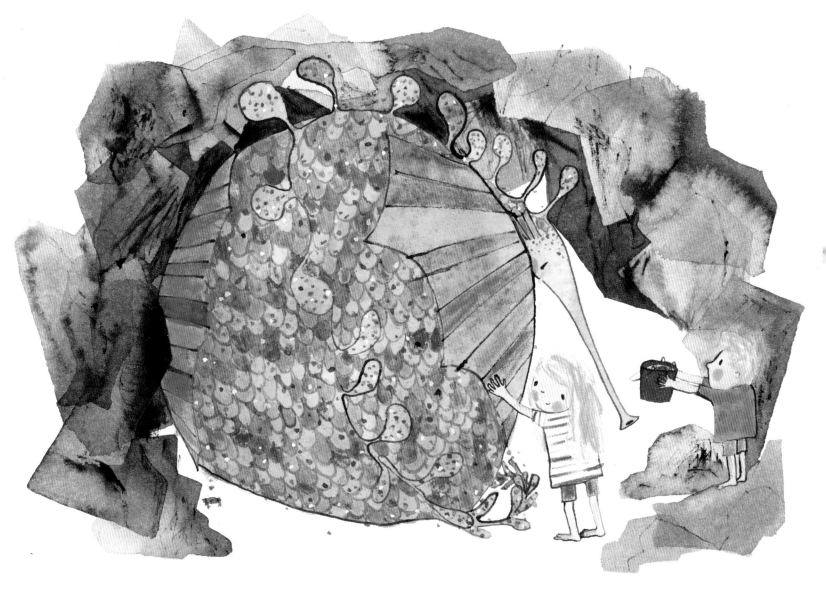

'I'm Amy,' said Amy. 'And I'm Callum.' But the lonely Sea Dragon wouldn't tell them his name. 'I think he's a bit scared of us,' whispered Amy.

The Sea Dragon was so big that he had to curl his tail all the way around his body to fit into the cave. He gazed out of the cave towards the sea.

'Can you swim?' Callum asked him.

'I'm a sea dragon,' said the Sea Dragon.

'What do sea dragons do?' asked Amy.

'They go on wild adventures,' boasted the Sea Dragon.

'Is that how you got lost?'

The Sea Dragon hid his head between his scaly paws and thumped his tail on the sand in anguish. Amy and Callum jumped back to a safe distance.

'We'd better put our crab back in the pool,' they said.

'I'm lost,' cried the Sea Dragon again. He didn't want Amy and Callum to leave him.

'You're not lost any more,' said Callum. 'We know where you are, and we're going to come and see you every day. But we have to go home for tea now.'

'Can I come too?' asked the Sea Dragon.

'I don't think you would like it,' said Amy. 'Goodbye for now, Sea Dragon. We'll come back in the morning.'

That night they lay awake and tried to think of ways to make the Sea Dragon happy. 'We could bring Petra down to play with him.' Petra was their dog.

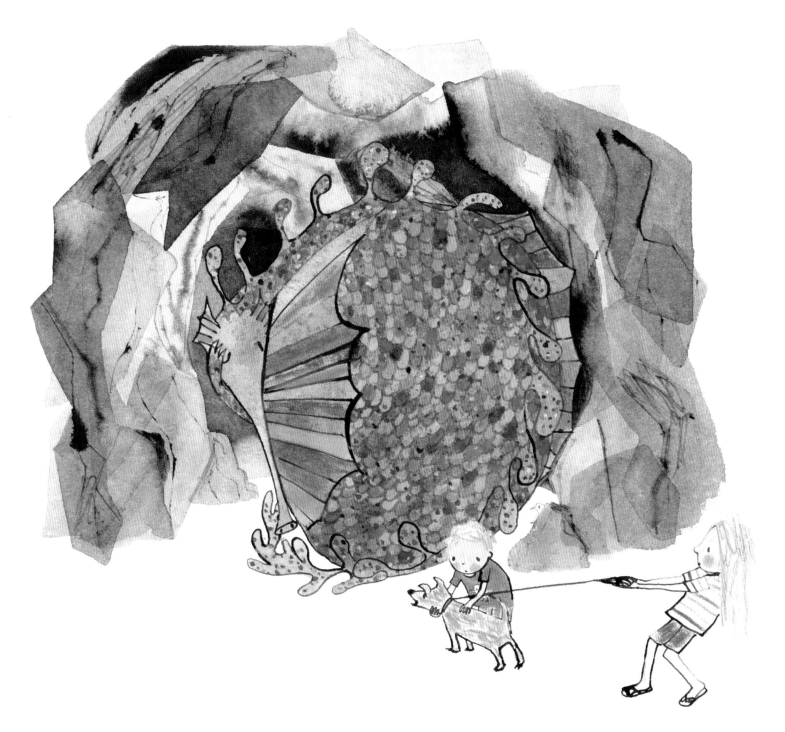

ut the Sea Dragon was scared of Petra when she jumped up and
barked at him. He screwed his eyes tight shut and made himself as
small as a sea dragon can be. Petra barked and barked until Amy and
Callum took her away.

'That wasn't a good idea,' said Amy.

'We could bring him an ice-cream,' said Callum.
They shook all the coins out of their money-boxes and went to the ice-cream kiosk. They showed the man their money and asked for the biggest ice-cream they could buy. It was a triple scoop with raspberry sauce and two chocolate flakes.

Very carefully, they carried the enormous ice-cream to the cave. The Sea Dragon stared at it and his eyes grew bright. He stretched out his long, dragonish tongue and the raspberry sauce, the chocolate flakes and the luscious creamy scoops of ice-cream vanished in one gulp. 'He didn't even lick it!' said Callum.

The Sea Dragon thumped his tail on the sand.
'More ice-cream!' he roared, but Amy and Callum had no money left.
The Sea Dragon wept big tears of disappointment.
'That wasn't a good idea,' said Callum.

'I think he needs a toy,' said Amy.
'What kind of toy do sea dragons play with?'
'Maybe a balloon?'

Their friend the balloon seller gave Amy and Callum a purple and silver balloon. They ran all the way to the cave with the balloon bobbing high in the air on its long string. The Sea Dragon pushed the balloon with his snout. He breathed and the balloon floated up to the roof of the cave. He flicked his tail and the balloon danced.

'He likes it!' shouted Callum.

All day the Sea Dragon played with his balloon. When evening came he breathed as hard as a dragon can breathe, like this:

. . . and the balloon floated out of the mouth of the cave, high into the air, higher and higher until it was flying far away above the green and turquoise sea. Amy and Callum watched the balloon until they couldn't see it any longer. The Sea Dragon watched it too.

The Sea Dragon was always hungry. He ate all their sandwiches and crisps, and the chips with curry sauce they had on Friday nights as a treat. When Amy bought a bag of doughnuts with her pocket money, the Sea Dragon scoffed them all.

'He's rather greedy, isn't he?' she whispered to Callum, but the
Sea Dragon overheard.
'You'd get hungry, if you were as lonely as me,' he said lugubriously, and tears began to slide down his turquoise scales.
'Don't cry,' said Amy, 'I didn't mean it.'

Amy and Callum loved the Sea Dragon more each day. He was so beautiful and he needed them so much. He didn't have anyone else. 'We're your friends,' they told him.
Amy brought a soft cloth from the kitchen, and she polished the Sea Dragon's scales until they glittered and gleamed. The Sea Dragon curled his tail around Amy and Callum, and told them stories of his wild adventures.
'Do you think they're true?' whispered Callum, and Amy shook her head.
'But don't let him know we know,' she said. 'We don't want to hurt his feelings.'

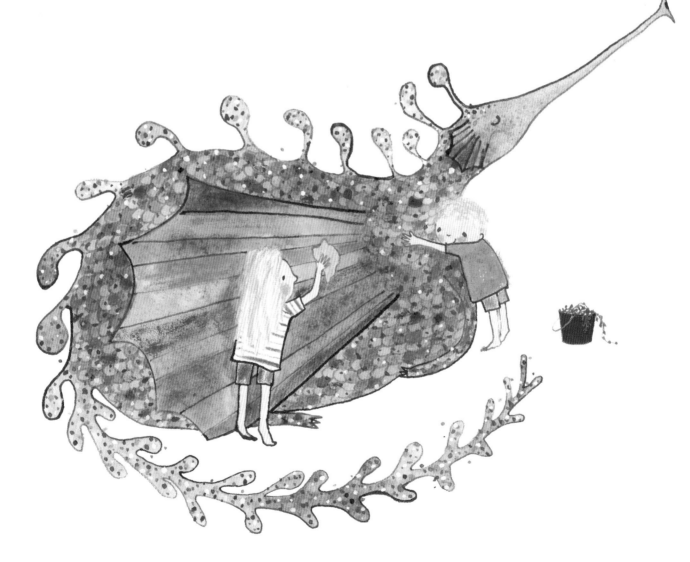

The nights were getting longer and the days were growing cooler. Summer was coming to its end. Soon school would begin and what would the Sea Dragon do then, without Amy and Callum?

'What are we going to do?' asked Amy. 'Even if we come every day after school, he will be alone for hours and hours. He will be so lonely.'

'And so hungry,' said Callum.

'He needs us so much,' said Amy.

Callum stared hard at the Sea Dragon. His exquisite turquoise-scaled dragon snout pointed at the open sea. His eyes were full of longing. 'What are you looking at, Sea Dragon?' Callum whispered. The Sea Dragon didn't turn his head. He didn't want to look away from the sea. The sea is his home, thought Callum. That's why he can't be happy here. The wild waves broke into foam, and a single tear slid down the Sea Dragon's scales.

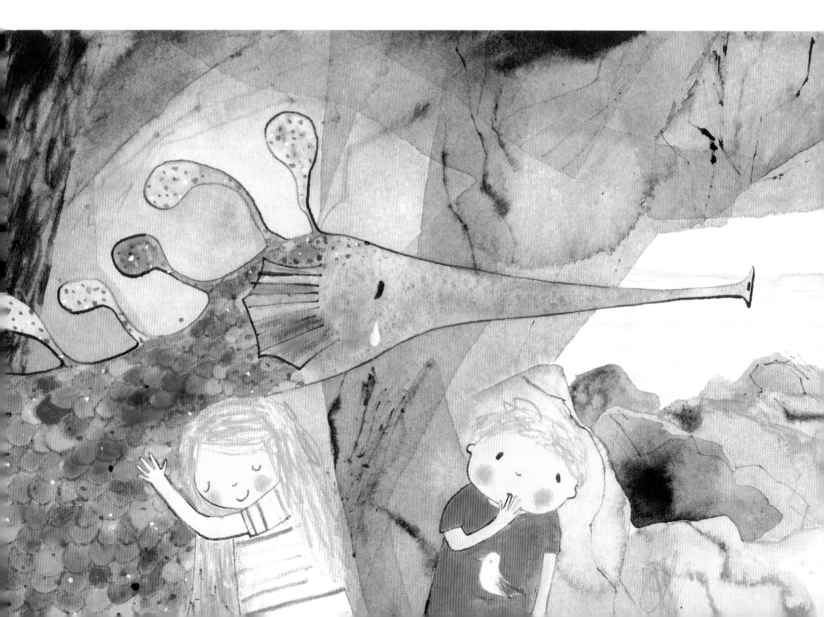

'We can't leave him alone here,' said Amy. 'He needs us.'
But Callum shook his head. 'I don't think the Sea Dragon needs us any more, Amy,' he said.
'Of course he does! We look after him. We love him.'
'He needs the other sea dragons,' said Callum. 'He needs his friends and relations.'

That night, Amy and Callum could not sleep. They kept thinking about the Sea Dragon's friends and relations.

'I don't think he's a grown up sea dragon,' said Amy. 'Maybe that's why he cries so much.'

'But he's so big,' said Callum.

'He's little inside,' said Amy.

'Then maybe they are searching for him,' said Callum. 'Maybe that's why he keeps looking at the sea, in case they come for him.'

Next day Amy and Callum went to the sea's edge. They shaded their eyes and stared at the sparkling waves. Were there other sea dragons out there?

'If there's one sea dragon, then there must be others,' said Callum. 'He can't be the only one in the world.'

'Do you think the other sea dragons would come if he called to them?' asked Amy.

'They won't hear him calling from inside the cave,' said Callum 'It's too far from the sea.'

'I know!' said Amy, 'Let's take him down to Lowena Rocks! The water's deep enough there for the other sea dragons to come in and fetch him.'

They shaded their eyes and stared out at Lowena Rocks. The dark rocks made the shape of a dragon. Maybe a sea dragon.

'It's definitely the right place,' said Callum.

'It's time to go on a wild adventure,' said Callum to the Sea Dragon. It was very early in the morning, and the day was rough and rainy. There was no-one on the beach. There was no-one to glimpse the Sea Dragon. 'We're going to find your friends and relations,' said Amy.

It was a wild walk to Lowena Rocks. The Sea Dragon shrank against Amy and Callum as if he were afraid of the big world outside the cave. But then the wind blew harder and the salt spray touched his skin. He lifted his head and lolloped over the rough dark rocks, down towards the water. Now Amy and Callum had to run to keep up with him. Soon they were at the edge of the boiling sea.

'Call to them!' shouted Callum against the noise of the wind.

The Sea Dragon raised his head. His voice came out in a roar like the breaking waves. It was so loud that Amy and Callum clapped their hands over their ears.

'His friends and relations will hear that for sure,' said Amy.

The waves rushed in, and under the white foam there was blue and green and turquoise.

'Sea dragons,' breathed Amy and Callum.

Their Sea Dragon gripped the very edge of the rock with his claws, and looked down. His body quivered. It was a long way down from the rock to the water. The sea made a noise like a lion as it burst against Lowena Rocks. Maybe the lonely Sea Dragon was scared, thought Amy.

'Go, Sea Dragon, go!' she shouted. 'Your friends and relations are waiting for you.'

The Sea Dragon bunched up his tail. A big wave was coming. In one quick, dragonish rush he sprang from the rock to the water. The sea closed over him and he disappeared.

'He didn't say goodbye,' said Callum.

'He didn't have time,' said Amy.

They shaded their eyes and stared into the waves. They could see blue and green, turquoise and sparkling silver. The tide was turning. It was going out, and all the sea dragons were going with it.

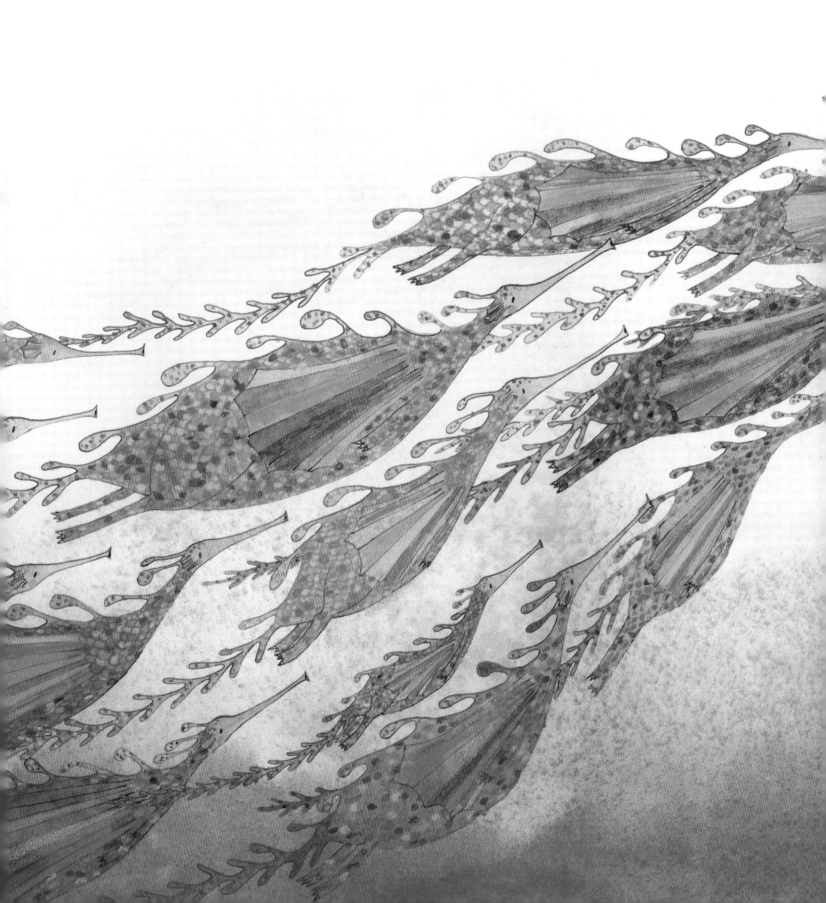

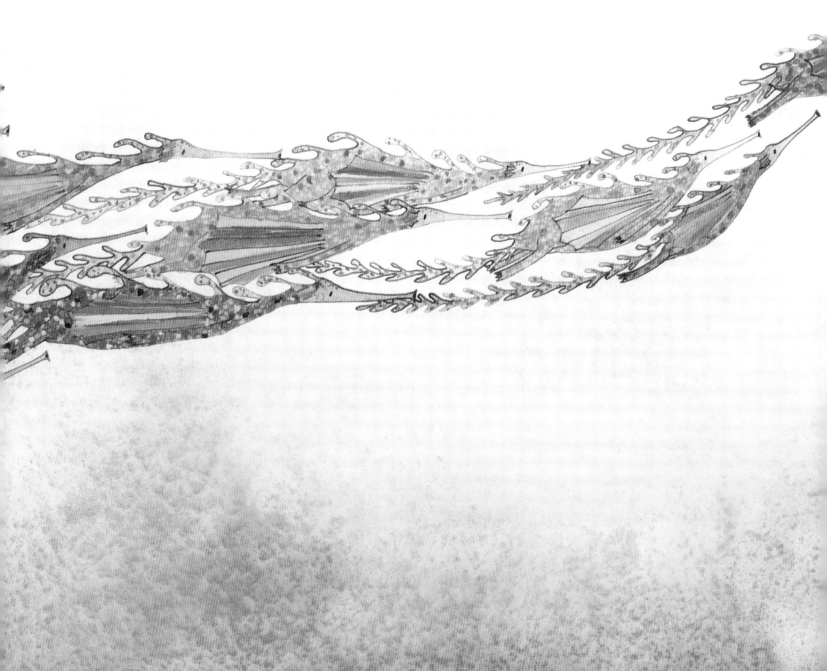

he Sea Dragon swam through the wild water with his friends and relations. He had forgotten what lonely meant.

Amy and Callum filled a small glass bottle from the pool of the Sea Dragon's tears. They stoppered the bottle with a cork stopper, and put it on the window sill of their bedroom.

Every morning, the tears gleamed blue and green and silver. They shone as bright as the Sea Dragon's scales.